Nursery Rhymes

Mary Had a Little Lamb

And Other Best-Loved Rhymes

ARCTURUS

This edition published in 2012 by Arcturus Publishing Limited
26/27 Bickels Yard, 151–153 Bermondsey Street,
London SE1 3HA

Copyright © 2012 Arcturus Publishing Limited

All rights reserved.

ISBN: 978-1-84858-680-2
CH002348US
Supplier 15, Date 0412, Print run 1756

Printed in China

Mary Had a Little Lamb

Mary had a little lamb,
Its fleece was white as snow,
And everywhere that Mary went,
The lamb was sure to go.

It followed her to school one day,
That was against the rule,
It made the children laugh and play,
To see a lamb at school.

So the teacher turned it out,
But still it lingered near,
And waited patiently about,
Till Mary did appear.

"What makes the lamb love Mary so?"
The eager children cry.
"Why, Mary loves the lamb, you know,"
The teacher did reply.

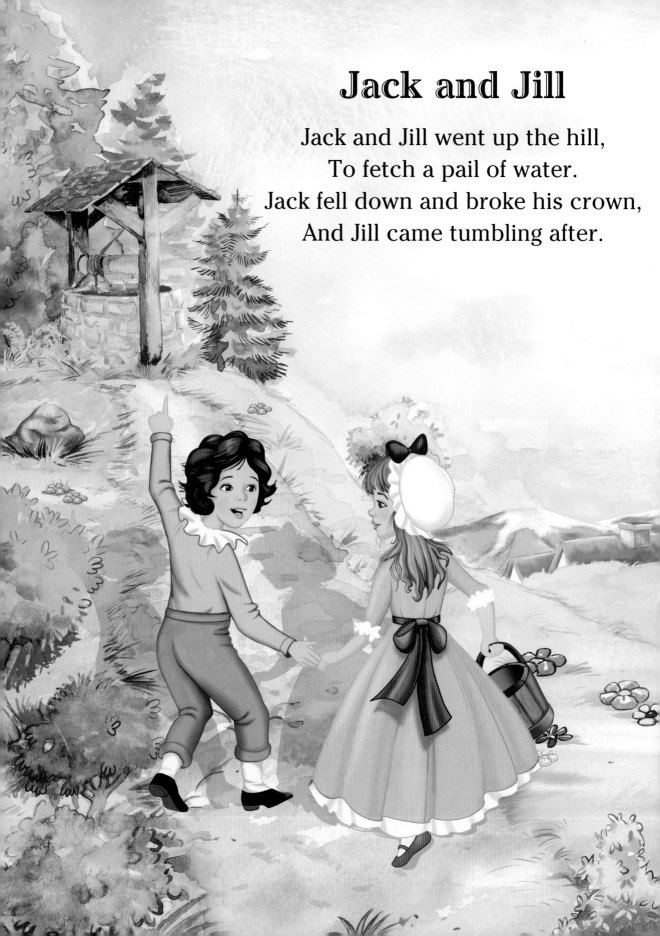

Jack and Jill

Jack and Jill went up the hill,
To fetch a pail of water.
Jack fell down and broke his crown,
And Jill came tumbling after.

Then up Jack got, and home did trot,
  As fast as he could caper,
Where his mother covered his head,
  With vinegar and brown paper.

Hot Cross Buns

Hot cross buns!
Hot cross buns!
One a penny, two a penny,
Hot cross buns!

If you have no daughters,
Give them to your sons;
One a penny, two a penny,
Hot cross buns.

Three Blind Mice

Three blind mice, three blind mice,
See how they run, see how they run!
They all ran after the farmer's wife,
Who cut off their tails with a carving knife.
Did you ever see such a sight in your life,
As three blind mice?

There Was an Old Woman Who Lived In a Shoe

There was an old woman
Who lived in a shoe.
She had so many children
She didn't know what to do.
She gave them some broth,
Without any bread,
Then kissed them all quickly
And sent them to bed.

Cock-a-Doodle-Do!

Cock-a-doodle-do!
My dame has lost her shoe,
My master's lost his fiddle-stick

And knows not what to do.
Cock-a-doodle-do!
What is my dame to do?
Till master finds his fiddle-stick,
She'll dance without her shoe.

Peter Piper

Peter Piper picked a peck of pickled peppers.
A peck of pickled peppers Peter Piper picked.

If Peter Piper picked a peck of pickled peppers,
Where's the peck of pickled peppers
Peter Piper picked?

Star Light, Star Bright

Star light, star bright,
The first star I see tonight.
I wish I may I wish I might,
Have the wish I wish tonight.